LOVE DOESN'T HURT, LOVERS DO

Love doesn't hurt, Lovers do

Love doesn't hurt, LOVERS DO

By JJACQZ

Love doesn't hurt, LOVERS DO

Love doesn't hurt, LOVERS DO

Love doesn't hurt, LOVERS DO

Love doesn't hurt, LOVERS DO

CONTENTS

Intro

I wrote this book so you can feel your heartbeat.
So you can feel a breath down your neck
intense,
unavoidable.

So, you can feel what I felt
every time I second-guessed myself,
every tear that stretched from morning into afternoons end.

So, you can listen to every fear
and recognise it as your own.

I want to hold your hand
while I show you how love becomes a game,
how we learn the rules too late,
and how, in the end,
we learn how to walk away
like we hadn't just unravelled ourselves.

I wrote this book for you.

4

But also, for me…

Because I don't follow the rules.
Because Tradition never spoke my language
Because freedom writes better poems than form ever could
Because I found healing in pieces and further hurting in others
Love is not linear; its timeless.
Like this book
It just is, it will just be
Like our emotions that bond together you and me
This book isn't meant to be read front to back
It's Meant to be felt, moments in, and moments out
Out of order, or all at once.

Almost finished the Bottle of Pink Moscato,
called him secretly in the middle of girls
night, to come pick me up....
for Lust ♡

6

I AM BARE.

I am bare.
I am a bear with no fur, just covered in fear
Feared that you won't like how tight this feels.
My naked chest, bare for you; my back arched like I have nine more
lives to fulfil
and in all of those 9 we try another round
to get you to the sounds I love to hear
when you whisper in my ear
and ask me, "Do you like that?"
I want you so close that you are my skin, and I let you copy my every
heartbeat that echoes yours,
I am a bear, with no fear when my legs are wrapped around your
waist, we
gravitate, every time and I place my finger down every line that is
ingrained on
your skin from my nails as I dig them in,
And you growl like the bear you are when you're about to finish, but
you place
back in, trying to bring me to the same amount of aggression that
brings us to sin.
I can't imagine a better place than this climax we are in- it is euphoric,
So, I slide down
and put my mouth all over it.

It starts off cliché.

You are my sunshine,
Once upon a time
I wanted to rise with you,
but I left before the sun came out,
I couldn't stand to see you in the day light,
For me I only wanted you in the night,
I only wanted to feel your head between my legs
And occasionally your hand.
I waited up for you to call me over.

Midnight.

"Are you a poet at midnight?" he asked.
I glared into his never-ending eyes,
through there, I watch the time we spend coming closer
to an end.
My heart shatters by the second…
I rest my fingers round his throat,
I utter, "Yes."
Because that's when you come through
And show me all the moves you intended to,
And I have to work my words around you
Before the next midnight falls,
And I fall in love all over again."

11

Him: "You love your photography innit…"

you're just my muse my eyes spoke

"Yes, I do!" My mouth muttered, as I licked my lips,

and the image of him spitting in my mouth that day returned.

12

LUST.

Imagine being touched in the spot that lust turns into
love.
And there is nothing you can do about it?
Just sigh.
While you fall head over for a man who didn't know
he touched you,
exactly how you needed him too.
And neither did you.

. . .

Romeo and Juliet

I hate you!

But I loved you more than I hated you,
So, when Juliet said my only love sprung from my only hate,
I knew you were my version of Romeo,
just not the same.

You fell in lust for me from the moment you saw me
But I wasn't young like her,
I was experienced and unruly.

I know you never saw true beauty until that night
Mine radiant.
And You whispered in my ear
'but soft, what light through yonder window breaks? It is the east, and you are the sun'.
Years later I grew to know you, to be the one.
And you, to know me to be amongst the other ones
so in the end I bled tears for us.
While our love withstood the betrayal, lies and deceit.
I wasn't happy.

So In the very end we were
Star crossed
but not in love
In lust.

14

Euphoria

I hoped the wind would blow you towards me,
On the cold nights, just so I can feel your warmth on those nights.
I'm caught, in a whirlwind of missing you,
especially on these lonely nights when I look up at the sky
and see you in the stars wrapped around it.
That's how I imagine the two of us-
Me, the pages of a book, covered in you
The title is "US" too,
I trust you,
to keep surging through like electricity,
I want to be the reason you light up,
every morning, every evening and every night.
I wouldn't mind switching with you;
Me, the switch,
You, the finger
as you press on my chest,
to feel my heartbeat for you.
Then you press again,
played like black and white keys
to make the sweetest melody,
on the grand piano,
Me, the keys,
You, the cover
as you lay on top of me silent at night,
and watch each other in the dark,
waiting to be risen like the sun,

Me, the sun,
You, the sky,
as I brush past you, and you smile at me too.
I want to be sprayed like perfume,
You, the neck,

Me, the particles
as I seep in your skin
And bring the warmest embraces in.
I want to tell you, you smell nice, and it's because of me
Can't you see?
I don't want to live without you.
I want us hand in hand like grains in the sand
that merge together to create the promise land,
that belongs to the seas.
You, the sea,
Me, the sand
and you visit me on the shore, we are never apart
you cover me, you make me wet with love and I drown in
you.
And you pick me up again like a plectrum,
You, the hands,
Me, the guitar strings
and you strike me accordingly.
I want to be played like Drum & Bass;
You,
the drum,
Me, the base
and we get drunk to the sounds of whatever we play,
and we dance the Meringue,

No, the Bachata. No, the Kizomba,
and our moves sensually kissing like lips.
And I close my eyes while we kiss till,
I sleep.
You, the dream,
Me, the memory,
and I can't wait to wake, to see you again.

18

"You don't know how to take a compliment."
he spoke.
"Describe what I do know how to take!"
I uttered breathlessly.

Peace.

I'm supposed to feel nothing but peace
when the thought of you arises,
but it passes with everything that doesn't include peace.
I'm supposed to feel peace when you lay your hand inside my thigh
but anxiety fills these sheets between you and I.
I was told not to give my all, to you. But I gave something close,
I realised now it was the wrong thing to do,
and I warned you, but no one warned me of the possibility
of losing myself being around you.
The lasting trauma of that, reflects on my soul, not yours.
I came to you for replenishment and energy saving,
but you sucked me clean and dry of the last energy I have left
to power both me and you.
That was the only time I thought your tongue was powerful.
Now, all I have is memories of you throbbing between my lips
and you not taking the time to please me,
then you selfishly rushed me away, as soon as you took what was
meant to stay
And I didn't know what to say,
But goodbye to you.

Put all our cute couples goals videos
Together with 'Hers & Hers' playing over it
In Love x

22

23

"How are you?" He asked.
I replied, *"I am love, how are you?"*
To which He responded *"I am strength"*
It was then I knew…

24

No question

He sat there and looked me dead in the eyes
And said.
"You love me!"
I asked him "How do you know?
I've never uttered those words to you."
He said.
"I know because I can feel it."
The strangest part is-
everybody else prior to him
would make me prove it.
I still till this day wonder what my love feels like?

26

My delusional illusion
engraved in the tree,
Your name with mine,
You with me.

She is art.

She is art.
Power beyond measure.
She has the ability to touch
you in places
you never imagined possible.
She may not be what the magazine considers beauty,
But her beauty concentrates on you,
And it rests between her ears
to see a different version of you.
Every time you move
She can paint a vivid picture
Without describing the physical you,
and She's right every time.
She notices every line
and every sigh,
She strokes you
all over,
Oil on canvas,
the canvas of your skin,
takes the depths of you in,
She exhales.
You take your first breathe.

12 things I love about you.

I hate that you are so attentive
and that you gravitate to my needs.
I hate that you pull my shoulders back every time
you notice my posture lean.
I hate that you have memorised what each and
every one of my facial expressions mean.
I hate that when you touch me,
I forget what hate means.
The little dance you do with your head and neck
then you smile,
I hate that too.
I hate all of you
And a little bit more.
I hate the way you kiss my forehead and ask me
what that means,
like I don't know it means 'amore',
I hate that I want you to continue, I hate that I
want some more.
More than anything I hate that I don't hate you, not
even close, not at all.

Imperfectly.

You're still searching for a perfect that doesn't exist
You'll continue to search and miss
instead of looking for the beauty in imperfection,
because that's where true perfection exists.

(I'll just throw it out there, I am (I'm)perfect.)

31

Rumi.

I crave a love that fears to lose me.
I cry for a love so tearful it replaces every drop in the ocean
And I drown.

I want to know how many tears of desperation for you it takes to fill the
entire sea
Just so I can know how much love I want to receive,
if we are exchanging pleasantries

I'm so glad I have never felt real unprovoked honest love
because I don't know if I can take real pain,
and have real hate in my heart for someone I love so much,
So deeply, the ocean feels jealousy for me
I felt that so deep I tattooed him on me.

32

I trace your silhouette on my page
filled with words from my fingertips.
Your name on my caller I.D,
each time I can't resist,
but to let you in.

34

The stars.

I told the stars about you,
they told me stay away.
"Every night he thinks about you,
but every other night his mind is away."
I didn't believe them anyway
So, I waited for the light of day,
but I knew deep down
the stars would never lead me astray.

Jack and Rose…

Love is stillness in motion.
And we sway on a yacht of love through
the skies reflected oceans.
And we dance at the bow
as we sail through this love
and into the next,
And here- after.

Love isn't just a word, It's a vibration.
And every touch we touched
Vibrated, the left ventricle that pumped
the blood from the atrium
It sounded like the beat of the drum when you rested on my chest,
And you touched there, 'did you feel the vibration?'

Motionless when I watch you staring back at me.
And I feel grounded like the anchor on my shoulder,
to represent you,
the helm to symbolise us
Steering through this love into different directions.

I trust you,
Even if it sinks,
I'm with you…

All I had to say about you,
was how beautifully you transitioned from your laugh to a
smile.

Or even better, when you transitioned from; Angry at me,
to a smile, because of me.

U-turn

I found someone else I could write about,
then I got tired
and my attention ran back to you,
Plus, my pen ran out of ink,
my hands got a little bit confused
we changed direction,
back to describing you.
It was like I took a U-turn in the road and
the destination took me back home.
To U

39

I'm fed up with thinking of you,
and wondering if you think of me too,
But I know you do, I see the finsta pop up

I know you saw mine too.

You are magic.

You are magic,
You are stars.
Your eyes like the moon entering eclipse
Your lips,
We kiss, and I get lost in the magic of what this could bring.
I fear if you let me in on the secret
I'll fall.
And I won't land on my feet
to be able to run away from you.
I won't escape,
I don't want to.
I'm mesmerized by those fingertips that you place between
mine,
Our hands locked in
like stars in the night.
They are supposed to be there,
Shining amongst one another.
I look up at you,
Your dark complex-skin
When you look away,
I'm mesmerized by the way you smile.
Your pearls,
You're perfect to me.
Don't look away, you will see perfection in the reflection of
my eyes
Look at me.

I saw you playing me, so I played too
had to put on The big boy shoes
For The Game!

On the other side.

Maybe I'm actually damaged, beyond repair,
maybe I'm not on the other side,
maybe I'm still on this side
trying to look in,
and I keep making the same mistakes again,
and racing to this thing called love that
I can't seem to win.
I wanted to believe I have healed this hurting
But the hurting keeps creeping back in.
I thought I closed the door to the that
And the next chapter I was in,
only showed me a new type of hurt
And also, how to hurt him.

Siren

I look at him from across the room,
and he draws closer to me,
infatuated by my glazed-over eyes, it's time to hypnotise.

Then I turned to you.
Drawn, the moment you look at me.
My greed for attaching you to me
doesn't allow your gaze to lose me.
You're lost in me.

Without a word, without a sound, without a touch,
I see you undress me. I can feel you breathe uncontrollably

But just like that
you open your mouth towards mine
and you lose me.

Then I bound my gaze towards someone else
and he falls harder, faster.
That excites me, this intensity,
the electricity. It flows through a current that electrocutes me

I own you.
My femininity mixed with masculinity enrages you.
You try to take control,
but my fingers press the X and O.

But you're not an anomaly.
Your touch I've felt before,
so I loosen my gaze
and set it upon someone new.

In this room I can have all of you.
Separately, I don't want any.

But I play the fiddle —
that's my siren sound.
And you all dance,
not physically, but through your energy.

It sparks something in you
that's within me.

I use these weapons that are my eyes
to draw you closer. And cast you away when I don't need you

I control the narrative
when I close my eyes
and open them
for someone new entirely.

And I burn down this fucking room.

I wish you all the best.

You had no control over me because I am already made,
Your opinion of me is weathered and out of date,
I never expected anything to go this far anyway.
They say the ones you decide to give a chance end up hurting
you anyway.
You fired the worlds amount of negativity at me
To try and break me.
But I told you,
I am already made from being broken, I cannot break again!

You laid your head to rest on my breast, you expressed how
much you missed me but I found out you kissed her the same
way you kissed me
so,
I hope you live happily ever after,
But,
stay away from me.

I sat there and lied.

I sat there in front of you and said
"You're the only one I'm talking to",
because I didn't want to hurt you.
I know how precious you are and
how much you wanted me to just be for you
But that wasn't possible.
You caught me right at the time where
My time, isn't even mine.
And as much as I tried to share a lot with you
they all required the same amount of time too,
and I loved it.
I was up with you until you couldn't be up no more, and I
had another waiting.
You asked me "Am I dating?"
and I said "No!"
but I wasn't ready for my heart to be naked
For me to bear my soul to you.
The truth is-
I had no reason to tell you.
and all this time I pressured you,
all while I was also lying too.
and what you did
I was doing too.
I knew you weren't here to stay,
So I played the same game you played.

There's more to this story…

I had a choice to make between the two of you;
The one that I chose, was the one to break me too.
The one I was in lust with
Was the one I thought I knew.
Little did I know would cause me damage too.

To add insult to injury
would make me number two.
Imagine, I had a choice between the one I believe is my soul mate
Vs the one the one I thought I knew,
But clearly, I didn't know any of them.

Anyway, YOUUUUUUUU

Towards the end.

I started to fall out of love with you
the moment you fell in love with me,
And it was hard to see you like that,
Because I hadn't received that amount of energy
when we were together.
from the moment we grew apart,
or I grew.
But I still held you close, almost every night,
but every other night my mind was with someone else.
I remember you asking me,
"Do you like him?" at my party,
and I lied and said "No!"
Just so I wouldn't hurt you,
but the truth is I did,
but I wasn't ready to let you go,
I wanted you to love me, but my love had already let go.

52

You are not what I wanted.

I was in love soulfully here and loathing physically there.
I sometimes think I fall for circumstance-
I fall because you are there,
not because I'm ready or willing to'
Or that it happens because the universe told me to,
but only because your persistency kept you there.
It was easy to become lost in you because,
you smothered me with what I wanted
at the time-
when no one else was around
and I didn't want to hurt you,
I knew me doing this would hurt me later on too.
So, I guess we are equal.

54

Let go.

You know I never actually wanted to be with you
I just felt compelled to say I do.
This wasn't no match made in heaven
I knew we weren't compatible,
it was just passionately fruitful at times
that turned stale many times,
And I continued on for a year,
because I liked how liberating it felt.
Especially when you run your hand down my arm
and held my hand,
Those motions are what made me fall for you,
when we handheld it was those times, I didn't want to let go
but every other time, I promise you, I was ready for you to
go.

Took my whatsapp picture down.
Deleted my instagram. Started posting
quotes of Heartbreak. :)

Love almost killed me

I smiled for the last time, I didn't know it would be.
As you loosened your grip, I saw a look on your face
I knew this was it, but I stayed delusioned in believing we are meant to be

I tried to laugh it off, because I loved you,
And pretend this hurt didn't exist.
I let you kiss my forehead, and my mind went adrift

I didn't want to believe you didn't love me.
You were never present.
And I blamed myself for turning a blind eye—
feeling unworthy.
Maybe if I showed you how much I loved you,
you would pick me
And you raised the pain you knew you were about to cause
And plunged it in my chest,
And you held one hand, and twisted it in with the other
You wiped my tear, and said everything is okay, but I didn't feel okay
I was dying, in your hands,
like it wasn't you layed the force of death into my chest

It was a stake to the heart, and I bled till it drained out my veins
And into hardwood floor that stained red
As you turnt away, the tears in my eyes blurred my view of you
I convinced myself it isn't you
And I blamed love, I thought it love that betrayed me
But it was you

58

What they don't tell you about love, is that it isn't the one to blame,

it's the people who claim to love you,

that will do you worse than an enemy or the same.

Lies that wore love's face.

The love bombing was a serious threat—
one I should have treated like a warning.
Maybe then I wouldn't have ended up in this mess.

My mind lived in constant dread
over a person who once said
he was going to be there forever.

Someone I thought I needed to protect—
but it was me
who I needed to protect

Because the lies weren't just words,
they were weapons.

The gaslight was the grip,
the fuel to your fire,
the spark that lit the match.

Luckily, I left before it exploded.

Because the village I made out of myself—
the woman I built from soil and softness—
almost burned down with it.

I'm not the same girl you met.

Every attempt to weaken me
broke something in me, yes—
but that break became bricks.

And I admit:
at one point,
you had me exactly where you wanted me—
dependent on your calls,
smiling at your texts,
crying at our distance.

I didn't know then
what I know now:

You never loved me.

You loved the version of me
who loved you too much
to leave.

OVER AND OVER

I don't have anything left unsaid.

I wasn't anything to you
and I realise that now,
after you finally showed me
you.

Your true face.
The real you.

And six years of seeing someone
I thought I knew
turned out to be a hallucination.

I'm wiser for that now.

No one can pull the wool over me again.
I see you
for exactly who you are.

The liar.
The deceiver.
The devil in disguise.

you revealed your truth
the one I always knew,
but you made me question it.

You made me question *me*.

Question what was real.

You said you'd never marry her.

I asked—over and over—
until I stopped needing the answer.

Because in the end,
you married the same person
you told me
to stop thinking about.

Over and over.

Plant.

Watered plants create healthy leaves,
That's like me.

If there isn't any care in the way you take care of me,
How do you expect me pose by window beautifully?

My weeping ends, weep overdue tears
due to not being taken care of by you.
If it was the other way around,
you would blossom!
And you know this to be true because even if I met you
withered
I'd water you.

I require delicacy, just a little, so my stem can stand strong.
My spine entwines with yours like the vine
that climbs up from the root bed,
to support my stem that is yours-
to help you grow, to be with you forever.
To help fix my posture.

But-

You don't know how to take care of plants.

Lost
Lost in love,
Lost from self,
Lost- out of love,
Lost in the wild.

Locution.

I was willing to do anything for you, apart from
Use my words.
And you used my non-existent words against me,
Nothing rolled off my tongue,
And you played on words that I never used and
those word plays confused me.
A double-entendre,
mixed with double standards.
My actions louder than colloquy,
I digress to a now, more transparent discourse
and still you wouldn't trust me.
The love language you used
against me required affirmation,
but I, threw like confetti the other 4,
but you still wanted me to tell you.
But the one thing I asked to hear,
you couldn't affirm, that you love me.

67

Is there anything worse than wanting someone
That doesn't want you?
And you start to feel unworthy

Speak to me.

How is it that we stopped speaking a long time ago,
but I can still hear you speak to me?
How is it that we lost all forms of communication,
but we still manage to find one another communicating?
I thought I lost you forever,
but not at all it seems.
And sometimes I just wish you'd pick up the phone and call me.

it's you who cut me off, as I just couldn't bare to do that to you.

Love doesn't hurt.

Love doesn't hurt lovers do
LOVERS DO!
If it were just me and you,
You would hurt me again
I know you
and even though I have the heads up this time
The way I loved you
I know I would love you again
And you'd hurt me
Again
And
Again
And for that, love isn't the one to blame
Its you!

Lovers do…

But if I knew how much you intended to
I probably would have tried to do the same to you
In fact, my heart doesn't beat like that
I terribly loved you
And to the detriment of me
You saw through me,
You saw the vulnerability
And maybe yes you did love me
But I loved you more than I did me
And you loved you more than you did me
So, there was no balance in love
So, we became unsteady.

72

I wrote this book so you can feel my heart break.
So, you can feel my nails against your back as I scratch away
At all the energy I put into you
And then wash it away.
Like when you asked me what my biggest fear is
And I told you, if I lost my innocence and my love
And then you left, and took the other one with you.

73

Maybe I'm not worthy?

Maybe it's just that,
I'm not worthy
Of a love so strong it makes me question
If I am worthy.
Maybe I'm not meant to receive
the same kind of love I know I can give
Or even more.
Maybe I'm not worthy
Of any love at all.

My hearts protector.

I asked if you could protect me,
you thought I meant physically.
What I forgot to say was,
Can you protect me,
Spiritually, emotionally, and mentally?
Can you protect the heart that is mine for me?
From you?
Can I give it to you, but not to hold as yours?
But to protect it, from you!
Can you hold it like it's the most precious thing you have ever
seen?
Without giving yourself the ability to break it,
Without giving yourself the power over me.
Can you protect my heart from the very person that would
take it?
I'll ask you again,
Can you hold it forever and not feel like it belongs to you?
I want you to hold the very essence of me,
guard me against you!

Alive

Have you ever seen a wildfire inside a tree?

It doesn't burn on the outside or the leaves

That's me.

Damaged on the inside, while still growing leaves

Producing oxygen so you can breathe

Taking in all your co2, even if it messes with me

I ebbed and flowed with you

I believed in your love whilst scared of it too.

Now at least I know it was just me, keeping you alive,

that satisfied you.

76

...if I finally managed to open my heart out
the way you request me to,
it would still get ripped apart by you.
I'm not lost without you
I was lost with you.
I hid away how I felt for you
Because I knew you were going to tear me apart anyway.

90 minutes.

Red flag, but because I didn't wear my glasses
It seemed pink, like a pink heart
It had a point, that was sharp but
Remember I didn't have my glasses on, so it looked
kind of blunt. And it was flapping in the wind
On the corner of the pitch but it looked like a game I
could play…
So, I put my boots on and, played a good game
90minutes in I was injured, the pitch I saw was
actually a cliff and it took me 90days to get to the
edge and I fell headfirst
(you know those first three months be the sweetest)
What felt like 90s minutes was 90 days
And as I got closer to the edge I had already fallen.
I only realised at the bottom, when I was broken, and
the red flag at the top stayed intact.

79

Fear of losing you.

I never want to feel a love that capable of leaving
Like what is the point in that.
Even after the end of everything, my love still sparks at the thought of
you,
so the fact that you can take yours away from me,
Please keep it.
That's not the type of love I want,
Broken promises based on a broken you
I just want to hear that I love you too, forever
even if it's not with you.

80

You said, "I am here forever
I am not going anywhere"
Tell me why you lied?
Because
You're nowhere to be seen.
ANYWAY

Farewell x

82

I no longer search your name, I finally
deleted all our memories
For Growth

Love doesn't hurt, LOVERS DO

covered in scars, stories and filled with forgiveness

Love didn't break me.

I just unfolded a new version of me—
like origami,
unravelled to reveal a new reality,
a person I'd been waiting to be.

I just didn't realise.

I prayed for my heart to stop breaking,
all while it was reshaping
into someone
who doesn't need a lover.

Another half?
I didn't need one—
because I'm not a fraction.

I'm whole.

86

A man is not worth more than his word....

Love doesn't hurt, LOVERS DO

87

But Listen to your intuition, not an empty affirmation.

Arise

I am still hope-full in the hope of love,
even though you tried to take that from me,
I know I'm damaged now.
But a day will come,
when the hope I kept alive will Arise.
And take a hold of me

90

I'm not sure how capable I am of being wholly in love,
but I'm sure I can love in bouts
I can be in love in moments,

and moments out.

Tear.

I promise you
this is the last time I'll tell you to leave me,
I returned to you one last time to tell you
That I don't need you anymore.

I noticed When I searched for you, you didn't need me.
so I had to consider me too
you selfishly, only thought of you.

And I,
lay half my tears for you.

You knew the force in which you held me,
a little closer, stronger, longer...
Now I can silently break away from the force of you,
that forced me to stay.

Maybe, one day we can dance a little longer, laugh a little louder,
touch a little softer
but until that day,
Please tell me you don't want to stay.
Just so I can finally walk away!

93

1 Year later

I unblocked you after a year
Because I thought I healed,
I heard a sermon
Saying forgiveness is the only way to move on
Then I played this song
Fall in love- Victor Thompson
And it reminded me of you,
it pulled me to tears
I'm still healing from this hurting
It seems that's going to take years.

2 years later

Some of our mutual friends posted you on your birthday
And I clicked the tag to pree.
I don't recognise you anymore
My gaze doesn't come with the love I used to see
I blocked you quickly, so you didn't see me
I am not hurting any longer,
I'm just angry at me, for
Ever loving you and not knowing if you ever did me.

95

3 years later

Remember when you said you hope I'll never find love ever again
I still haven't
Your wish became the universes command I guess
But I'm cool with that, I'm focussed on me.
I don't look out for you anymore
So, I guess that's a plus for me

Lessons.

Time for me to let go of the love I lost at sea
Just to stop sinking with you
You're the greatest lesson I have learnt,
in a multitude of ways, my lessons with you came in waves
And the last one I drowned,
while trying to surf it with you.
That's not to say I don't miss you,
because every morning and every evening I do
But I graduated from the University of You.
So, the only love I have left is this book,
Since I left you.

98

Now I sit here happier than I've been in a while,
Even though I might check your posts or two,
There's nothing in me
That wants to be any closer to you.

Remember what you seek is seeking you,
And that heart you want to fill can only be filled by you.
100

<u>My Last Sentiment</u>

I have settled in knowing
That I have no regrets in giving, all that love that I gave,
To whom I gave
But what I do know is
In the end They will regret
Losing the love they gained.

****

They say love hurts,
but I don't agree
Love will never hurt you
The wrong person will

****

LOVE doesn't hurt; LOVERS do!

OUTRO: There Is No Manuscript to Love

Sometimes I think out loud.
I think with my words on the page, and it's almost like I'm creating the sickest
monologue on stage—
but really, it's just my imagination running wild again.
At times, I can't make sense of what's going on in my brain.
These thoughts tend to go off on tangents, and I just have to let them spill onto the
page—
without poetics, without meaning,
without a title,
without context.
Just what I'm feeling at the time,
what sounds right.

A lot of the time, it comes straight from the heart—
and that seems to be the most important part.
My love is very loud to me.
You know that saying, *"wear your heart on your sleeve"*?
Admittedly, I can seem nonchalant, even cold to some—
but that's just me protecting myself.
(I think.)

I show love in abundance, just not always in the expected ways.
Along the way, I've realised—it's all about perception.
How you *see* things will determine how you *feel* things.
There are five love languages.
Some intertwine.
Some need only one.
Others need all five.

That alone is hard to juggle
when the way I give love is based on how I feel—
how comfortable I am.
It can distort the receiver's perception of me,
of how they think I feel,
based on how *they* like to receive.

The thing about love is—it must be shared.
You can't keep it to yourself.
But we also crave a kind of reciprocity
that strokes our ego.
And I don't believe ego and love are friends.

That's how I came to write this chapter of my life.
In school, boys pretended to like me, so I would buy them stuff.
Because they knew I was a giver!
Behind my back they would call my ugly,
and tell the girls they are just using me
besides that I've always loved deeply.
I was in a long-term relationship from sixteen to twenty-four—
so I only learned the basic, innocent parts of love.
After that, I found a deeper sense of confidence within myself,
which allowed me to give *real* love—
a more adult kind of love.

One of the hardest battles I've faced
is learning how to receive love.

As I never really know what that looked like.
It's not as easy as just picking it up and carrying it with you.
Receiving love is a gift,
complicated and almost unnatural—
like something you need a manual for.

Still, I'm hopeful.
Hopeful for the thought of love.
And I hold onto that hope every time I meet someone new.
It's like my slate gets wiped clean on the outside,
but the journey continues on the inside.
Every bump I've hit along the way—up or down—
I haven't forgotten.
I've learned from each one.

I overthink.
I over love.
I reminisce daily.

I've had amazing moments with people I've connected with—
whether for minutes, weeks, months, or years.
Each one has taught me something about myself.
I've faced my biggest fears,
and I wouldn't take a single experience back.

I've learned patience.
And impatience.
I've learned my touch is unforgettable.
And that I've never received a touch so intense that I didn't want it to end—
and I've learned to be okay with that.

I've learned I tell lies.
And that I lie very well.
Sometimes, I even enjoy it—it gives me a strange thrill.

I've learned that I'm more emotional and sensitive than I let on,
even more than I knew myself.
But I also know—I don't need to soften to please someone else.

I've learned I carry a spiritual presence that can be overwhelming,
while pretending I don't really care.
That contradiction can be confusing—
and I admit, I send out mixed signals.

I'm not perfect.
I can be shallow, overconfident, overzealous—
but I'm also loving,
caring,
willing to learn,
willing to adapt and compromise for love.

I don't live in regret,
but I do live in the margins of hurt and worry—
especially in situations and situationships.

I've been navigating this journey to love for fifteen years,
and I still haven't found the final destination—
if that even exists.

I've settled in some places,
and been unsettled in others.
I've had my first taste of real love,
and real heartbreak,
wrapped in real pain.

I cry every time I remember that pain.
And honestly—I don't think I deserved it.

I've met my karmic partner,
my twin flame,
and I'm not sure about a soulmate.

But for now—
I vow to love myself
completely,
wholly,
abundantly,
unapologetically.

And I hope you do too.

There is no manuscript to love,
apart from this one
I wrote for you.

— Love,
Jjacqz

Question: Are you ever going to heal from your hurting?
Or are you going to punish me for that too??

A Note on the Visuals

The photographs in this book are not just stills, but scenes — fragments of a stage where love, lust, betrayal, and growth are performed in silence.

The images do not decorate the poems; they run alongside them, telling their own version of events.
Each frame is a gesture, a pause, a reach, a break.
Together, they become a silent play, unfolding as you turn the page.

This book is not only to be read.
It is to be *seen, remembered, and felt*.

At the end, the story continues —
the stills move.
The performance comes alive.

P.S....

4 years later

I hadn't seen you in 4 years,
And when I finally saw you,
I didn't feel an inch of love lost.
I just knew
From then,
You are the only person I've ever loved that loved me too,
and I'm so glad I lost you.

With gratitude to the dancers

Chanone Murday, Deniz kartal, Mitchell Unuoya

Thank you for carrying this story with your bodies.
Every step, every reach, every fall you performed
became another line of poetry.
You turned my words into movement,
and gave the stills a heartbeat.

scan the code, and the stills move.

the voice

- for the words on
  page that wasn't
  enough...

Because love
refused to be silent
- Scan for a full
experience.

Love doesn't hurt, LOVERS DO

LOVE DOESN'T HURT, LOVERS DO

113

Love doesn't hurt, Lovers do

www.ingramcontent.com/pod-product-compliance
Lightning Source LLC
Chambersburg PA
CBHW021331060726
47591CB00006B/1966